N.º 3.

★
ICONS

N.º 7.

Shells
&
Corals

And there are no other
collections in all of Europe
wherein so many rare pieces
are to be found

ALBERTUS SEBA

The copy used for printing belongs to the Koninklijke Bibliotheek, Den Haag.
Signature: 394B 28

COVER:
Chambered nautilus /Pearly nautilus (decorated)

ENDPAPERS:
Precious corals

PAGES 2–3
Poisonous cone shells

PAGES 4–5
Spindles, crown shells and turrid shells

PAGES 10–11
Spider conchs or lambis shells

PAGES 14–15
Thorny oysters, Lazarus jewel boxes and a coral

PAGES 18–19
Scallops

© 2004 TASCHEN GmbH
Hohenzollernring 53, D–50672 Köln
www.taschen.com

Edited by Petra Lamers-Schütze, Cologne
Design by Claudia Frey, Cologne
Production by Ute Wachendorf, Cologne

Captions by Sven-Erik Engmann, Nina Hehn, Jes Rust,
Francisco Welter-Schultes, Rainer Willmann

English translation: Anne Hentschell (introduction),
Malcolm Green (captions)
French translation: Anne Charrière (introduction),
Yves Finet and Peter Schuchert (captions)
Spanish translation: José García

Printed in Italy
ISBN 3–8228–3252–9

ALBERTUS SEBA

Shells
&
Corals

*Muscheln & Korallen · Coquillages & Coraux
Moluscos & Corales*

TASCHEN

KÖLN LONDON LOS ANGELES MADRID PARIS TOKYO

ALBERTUS SEBA'S *collection of natural specimens and its* PICTORIAL COLLECTION

IRMGARD MÜSCH

By becoming an apothecary, Albertus Seba, who was born in 1665 in the East Frisian town of Etzel, chose a profession with close ties to natural history. Unlike today, medications were not synthetically made but mixed together from natural constituents. A whole range of traditional recipes were available to those versed in the art of creating remedies from animal, vegetable and mineral ingredients. But many did not stop there. They continued the search for new methods, collecting natural specimens from distant lands, studying them, and testing their potential uses. Their passion for collecting and researching often extended beyond immediate pharmaceutical applications. In many instances apothecaries started major natural history collections and contributed personally to the growing knowledge of nature.

With his "Die Deutsche Apotheke" (German Apothecary's Shop), as he called his business, Seba rapidly earned an excellent reputation for himself. Financially, too, he was successful – something which would enable him to establish his comprehensive collection of natural specimens. Not relying solely on casual customers who happened to pass by his apothecary, Seba actively sought them out. He traded in drugs from overseas, advertising his prices in an Amsterdam newspaper. He supplied departing ships with cases of medicines and treated their crews. It is related how, whenever a ship arrived in port, Seba would hasten down to the harbour without delay and administer his medicines to the exhausted sailors. Any natural specimens that they had brought with them he would then be able to purchase at a good price or accept in exchange for his medications.

In Amsterdam, Seba was ideally situated for starting such a collection of natural curios and he succeeded in assembling a wealth of natural specimens whose fame spread beyond the bounds of Amsterdam.

ALBERTUS SEBA'S THESAURUS

On 30 October 1731 a contract was signed in Amsterdam between three parties: Seba and the agents of two publishing houses agreed to produce a major work of 400 plates depicting Seba's collection. Ultimately, the Thesaurus incorporated a magnificent 446 plates, 175 of them double-page. The four volumes appeared over a span of 30 years, from 1734–1765. The commentary on the plates was published in a Latin-French and a Latin-Dutch edition, so as to reach a broad international readership of natural historians, collectors and book lovers. Seba wrote the text for the first two volumes largely himself, but also had other naturalists assist him. Volume I of the

Thesaurus opens with a few pages devoted to illustrations of the plant skeletons that Seba had prepared and conserved using his own special technique. These are followed by depictions of plants and animals from South America and Asia. Alongside lizards, birds, frogs, spiders and other creatures, Seba includes a few fantastical creatures, such as dragons. Volume II is dedicated primarily to snakes, but a few plants and other animals are also depicted on the plates for decorative purposes and in order to illustrate the reptiles' environment. Volume III is devoted to marine life. The imposing variety of sea creatures includes scallops, starfish, squid, sea urchins and fish. Volume IV presents, in nearly 100 plates, a large collection of insects followed by a few pages of minerals and fossils from Seba's cabinet.

Publication of a work like the Thesaurus called for considerable sums of money. Hugely expensive to produce were above all the many illustration plates, whose engraving was a laborious and drawn-out task. The names of no less than 13 artists are recorded as being employed on the transferral of the drawings, frontispiece, and portrait to the copperplates. The expensive work was initially published in black-and-white. It is not known whether the publishers also offered a hand-painted edition, which would naturally have raised the price and profit margin considerably. Buyers probably had the work painted at their own extra expense by specialist colourists. The gorgeous colours add substantially to the attractiveness of the plates, but their purpose was not just aesthetic enhancement. They had a scientific use as well. Some specimens, such as those of butterflies, snakes and shellfish, are only distinguishable by their colouring, and the differences in patterning of many fauna can barely be discerned in black-and-white. Whether or not originally in colour, whether or not based on existing illustrations, the Thesaurus remains an impressive example of a Baroque book. The illustrations in the second, third and fourth volumes, which rely much less on previously published sources, increasingly follow contemporary conventions in scientific literature. For best possible visual clarity, the animals are portrayed without any overlapping and with their size ratios correct – albeit in mirror image, which in the case of snail shells spiralling counter-clockwise became the source of some confusion. What was retained, though, was an ornamental arrangement of the objects on the plates, which is demonstrated by the symmetrically arranged snake plates as well as by artistically arranged shells and insects. Just as with the collection, there were thus always two aspects to the illustrations: they served both scientific instruction and aesthetic appreciation.

The Thesaurus treated an important collection of natural specimens of the early 18th century. As a book, the actual stationary collection became mobile and permanently accessible to many interested persons – even when the collection itself had long been scattered to the four winds.

This publication presents a representative selection of the most beautiful shells and corals from the third volume of the complete edition.

ALBERTUS SEBA'S *Naturaliensammlung* und ihr BILDINVENTAR

IRMGARD MÜSCH

Albertus Seba, 1665 im ostfriesischen Etzel geboren, wählte mit dem Apothekerberuf eine Profession, die zu seiner Zeit eng mit naturhistorischen Studien verknüpft war. Medikamente wurden nicht wie heute synthetisch hergestellt, sondern aus natürlichen Bestandteilen gemischt. Um aus Tieren, Pflanzen und Mineralien Heilmittel zu gewinnen, stand Arzneikundigen eine ganze Reihe überlieferter Rezepte zur Verfügung. Viele suchten jedoch nach neuen Wegen, sammelten Naturalien aus allen Himmelsrichtungen, studierten sie und erprobten ihre mögliche Verwendbarkeit. Vielfach verselbstständigte sich die Sammel- und Forscherleidenschaft über einen unmittelbaren pharmazeutischen Nutzen hinaus. Mehrfach legten Apotheker bedeutende naturhistorische Sammlungen an und trugen selbst zur wachsenden Kenntnis der Natur bei.

Mit seinem Geschäft, das er „Die deutsche Apotheke" nannte, erwarb sich Seba rasch einen guten Ruf. Zu dem großen finanziellen Erfolg seiner Apotheke, der ihm das Anlegen seiner umfangreichen Naturaliensammlung ermöglichte, trug ganz wesentlich bei, dass sich der geschäftstüchtige Seba nicht nur auf Laufkundschaft verließ. Vielmehr handelte er auch mit pharmazeutischen Rohstoffen (Drogen) aus Übersee, für die er unter Angabe der Preise in einer Amsterdamer Zeitung warb. Außerdem lieferte er den auslaufenden Schiffen Reiseapotheken und behandelte die Seeleute. Der Überlieferung zufolge eilte Seba unverzüglich auf die in den Hafen einlaufenden Schiffe und behandelte die Matrosen mit seinen Arzneien. Dabei gelang es ihm, den erschöpften Männern Naturalien, die sie mitgebracht hatten, günstig abzukaufen oder gegen Medikamente einzutauschen.

Mit Amsterdam hatte sich Seba einen Standort für den Aufbau einer Naturaliensammlung ausgesucht, wie er ihn besser kaum hätte finden können und es gelang ihm, eine bedeutende Sammlung aufzubauen, deren Ruf über die Grenzen Amsterdams hinausging.

DER THESAURUS VON ALBERTUS SEBA

Am 30. Oktober 1731 schlossen in Amsterdam drei Parteien einen Vertrag: Vertreter zweier Verlage und Seba vereinbarten darin, das Kabinett des Sammlers in einem großen Werk mit etwa 400 Tafeln zu publizieren. Tatsächlich umfasst der Thesaurus stolze 446 Tafeln, davon 175 als Doppelseite. Die vier Bände erschienen in einem Zeitraum von 30 Jahren, von 1734–1765. Die begleitenden Erläuterungen zu den Tafeln wurden jeweils in einer lateinisch-französischen und einer lateinisch-niederländischen Fassung veröffentlicht, da sich Seba mit dem Thesaurus an ein internationales Publikum von Naturforschern, Sammlern und Buchliebhabern wandte. Den Text der ersten beiden Bände verfasste Seba weitgehend selbst, doch ließ er sich von anderen Naturforschern unterstützen. Am Anfang des ersten Thesaurus-Bandes stehen zunächst einige Seiten mit Abbildungen von Pflanzenskeletten, die Seba mit seiner speziellen Präparationstechnik bearbeitet und konserviert hatte. Dann folgen Darstellungen von Tieren und Pflanzen aus dem südamerikanischen und asiatischen Raum. Neben Eidechsen, Vögeln, Fröschen, Spinnen und anderen Tieren finden sich auch einige Fabelwesen wie Drachen. Band II gilt vorrangig den Schlangen, zu dekorativen Zwecken und zur Veranschaulichung der Lebensweise der Reptilien sind allerdings auch einige Pflanzen und andere Tiere auf den Tafeln zu sehen. Dem maritimen Lebensraum ist der dritte Band gewidmet: Es erwartet den Betrachter eine überwältigende Vielzahl von Meerestieren wie Muscheln, Seesterne, Tintenfische, Seeigel und Fische. Der abschließende Band präsentiert auf knapp 100 Tafeln eine umfangreiche Sammlung von Insekten, gefolgt von einigen Seiten mit Darstellungen der Mineralien und Fossilien aus Sebas Kabinett.

Das Unterfangen, ein Werk wie den Thesaurus herauszugeben, erforderte beträchtlichen Einsatz von Geldmitteln. Vor allem die vielen Bildtafeln, deren Anfertigung mit hohem Zeitaufwand verbunden war, verursachten immense Kosten. Allein 13 Künstler, die Tafeln, Frontispiz und Porträt auf Druckplatten übertrugen, sind namentlich bekannt. Das teure Werk erschien zunächst in schwarz-weißer Ausführung. Es ist nicht bekannt, ob auch die Verlage selbst eine kolorierte Ausgabe anboten, die den Preis und die Gewinnspanne natürlich erheblich gesteigert hätte. Vermutlich ließen die Käufer das Werk auf eigene Rechnung farblich fassen und wandten sich dazu an spezialisierte Koloristen. Die Farbenpracht der Tafeln ist ein besonderer Genuss, doch erhöhte die Kolorierung nicht nur den ästhetischen Reiz, sondern auch den wissenschaftlichen Nutzen. Beispielsweise lassen sich manche Exemplare von Schmetterlingen, Schlangen oder Muscheln nur mit Hilfe der Farbe unterscheiden, während in Schwarz-Weiß die Unterschiede in der Musterung mancher Tiere kaum auszumachen sind. Mit oder ohne Kolorierung überzeugt der Thesaurus in jedem Fall als ein beeindruckendes Beispiel barocker Buchkunst. Die Tafeln des zweiten bis vierten Bandes entsprechen zunehmend einer zeitüblichen wissenschaftlichen Präsentation. Die Tiere sind – fein säuberlich nach Gattungen getrennt – aufgereiht. Für eine größtmögliche Lesbarkeit der Abbildungen sind die Tiere ohne Überschneidungen und mit einheitlichem Größenmaßstab abgebildet – allerdings seitenverkehrt, was bei Schnecken mit linksdrehendem Gehäuse zu Missverständnissen führte. Erhalten blieb eine ornamentale Anordnung der Objekte auf den Tafeln, die sich bei symmetrisch ausgerichteten Schlangentafeln ebenso zeigt wie bei kunstvoll arrangierten Muscheln oder Insekten. Somit enthalten die Illustrationen wie die Sammlung immer zwei Aspekte: Sie dienen gleichzeitig der wissenschaftlichen Belehrung und dem ästhetischen Vergnügen.

Der Thesaurus erschloss ein bedeutendes Naturalienkabinett des frühen 18. Jahrhunderts. Die eigentlich stationäre Sammlung wurde als Buch beweglich und für viele Interessenten dauerhaft verfügbar – auch dann noch, als die Sammlung selbst schon Jahrzehnte in alle Winde zerstreut war.

Der vorliegende Band zeigt eine Auswahl der prächtigsten Muscheln und Korallen des 3. Bandes der Originalausgabe.

N.º 2.

N.º 4.

N.º 6.

N.º 6.

N.º 7.

N.º 7.

N.º 9.

N.º 10.

N.º 11.

N.º 11.

N.º 4.

N.º 5.

N.º 5.

N.º 9.

N.º 8.

N.º 8.

N.º 10.

N.º 12.

N.º 12.

La collection d'histoire naturelle d'ALBERTUS SEBA
et son INVENTAIRE ILLUSTRÉ

IRMGARD MÜSCH

En devenant apothicaire, Albertus Seba, né en 1665 à Etzel, dans la partie orientale de la Frise, avait choisi une profession qui était étroitement liée à l'étude de l'histoire naturelle. Les médicaments ne s'obtenaient pas par synthèse, mais à partir de composants naturels. Pour tirer leurs remèdes des règnes animal, végétal et minéral, les connaisseurs disposaient de toute une série de recettes transmises par la tradition. Mais beaucoup cherchaient des manières nouvelles d'opérer, et collectionnaient à cet effet des objets de la nature en provenance des quatre coins du monde, dont ils étudiaient et testaient les usages possibles. Bien souvent, cette passion de collectionneur et de chercheur dépassait son utilité pharmaceutique immédiate. Il n'était pas rare de voir des apothicaires constituer d'importantes collections d'histoire naturelle et contribuer ainsi à une connaissance toujours plus grande de la nature.

Son entreprise, que Seba appela « La pharmacie allemande », lui valut rapidement une bonne réputation. Son habileté en affaires valut à Seba l'énorme succès financier grâce auquel il a pu payer son importante collection d'objets naturels. Evidemment, il ne se contentait pas seulement de la clientèle de passage. Il s'était aussi lancé dans le commerce des matières premières pharmaceutiques (drogues) d'outre-mer, dont il faisait la publicité dans une revue d'Amsterdam, en y indiquant les prix. Par ailleurs, il fournissait des pharmacies de voyage aux bateaux en partance et soignait les marins. Certaines sources racontent qu'il se précipitait au port à l'arrivée des bateaux, pour traiter les matelots avec ses remèdes. Il parvenait ainsi à acheter à bon prix à ces hommes épuisés des objets de la nature ou à les échanger contre des médicaments.

En s'installant à Amsterdam, Seba n'aurait guère pu trouver un lieu plus propice à la constitution d'une collection d'histoire naturelle et il réussit à constituer une collection imposante dont la renommée dépassa les frontières d'Amsterdam.

LE THESAURUS D'ALBERTUS SEBA

Le 30 octobre 1731, un contrat tripartite fut conclu à Amsterdam : les représentants de deux éditeurs et Seba convinrent de publier le contenu du cabinet de l'apothicaire dans un grand ouvrage d'environ 400 planches. Effectivement, le Thesaurus arbore 446 planches, dont 175 sous forme de double page. Les quatre volumes sont parus en l'espace de 30 ans, de 1734 jusqu'en 1765. Les explications qui accompagnaient les planches étaient chaque fois publiées en deux versions : l'une latino-française, l'autre latino-néerlandaise. En effet, Seba s'adressait avec son Thesaurus à un public international de naturalistes, de collectionneurs et de bibliophiles. Le texte des deux premiers volumes fut, dans une grande mesure, écrit par Seba lui-même, mais il se fit aider par d'autres naturalistes. Les quelques pages au début du premier volume du Thesaurus présentent des reproductions de squelettes de plantes, que Seba avait préparés et conservés à l'aide d'une technique spéciale. Les images suivantes étaient des représentations d'animaux et de plantes d'Amérique du Sud et d'Asie. Outre des lézards, des oiseaux, des grenouilles, des araignées et d'autres espèces, il représenta aussi des animaux légendaires, tels que les dragons. Le deuxième volume est avant tout consacré aux serpents, mais quelques plantes et animaux figurent également sur ses planches, à des fins décoratives et pour représenter la façon de vivre des reptiles. Le milieu marin fait l'objet du troisième volume où un nombre impressionnant d'animaux tels que coquillages, étoiles de mer, pieuvres, oursins et poissons attendent le lecteur. Le dernier volume présente sur une centaine de planches une vaste collection d'insectes, suivie sur quelques pages de représentations des minéraux et fossiles du cabinet de Seba.

La publication d'une œuvre telle que le Thesaurus nécessita d'importants moyens financiers. Surtout, les nombreuses planches, dont la réalisation demanda beaucoup de temps, générèrent des coûts immenses. Ainsi connaît-on les noms de pas moins de 13 artistes, qui transférèrent sur plaques les planches, le frontispice et le portrait. Cet ouvrage luxueux parut d'abord en noir et blanc. Nous ignorons si les éditeurs eux-mêmes ont proposé une version colorée, ce qui aurait évidemment considérablement augmenté le prix et la marge bénéficiaire. Il est probable que les acheteurs faisaient colorier leur livre à leurs propres frais, et qu'ils s'adressaient à cet effet à des coloristes spécialisés. La beauté des couleurs offre un plaisir particulier. Mais outre l'attrait esthétique, ce coloriage revêtait aussi une utilité scientifique. Par exemple, certains spécimens de papillons, de serpents ou de coquillages ne se distinguent que par leurs couleurs, et les différences de motifs ne sont guère visibles en noir et blanc.

Avec ou sans couleur, reprenant des images existantes ou non, le Thesaurus est en tout cas un exemple impressionnant et convaincant de l'art baroque du livre. Les planches des volumes deux à quatre correspondent de plus en plus à une présentation scientifique caractéristique de l'époque. Les animaux sont présentés les uns après les autres – soigneusement séparés par genre. Pour rendre les illustrations aussi lisibles que possible, les animaux ne se recouvrent jamais et leurs grandeurs respectives sont respectées. Il reste le principe de l'arrangement ornemental des objets sur les planches, que l'on observe aussi bien sur les illustrations de serpents à structure symétrique qu'avec les coquillages ou les insectes disposés avec art. Ainsi, les illustrations et les collections présentent toujours un double intérêt : l'instruction scientifique et le plaisir esthétique.

Le Thesaurus a fait découvrir au public un important cabinet d'histoire naturelle du début du XVIIIe siècle. Grâce au livre, la collection qui était stationnaire à l'origine, est devenue mobile et accessible à un large public d'intéressés, pendant encore des décennies après avoir été dispersée à tous vents.

Cette publication présente un choix représentatif d'illustrations de coquillages et de coraux du troisième volume de l'édition originale.

N.º 17.

N.º 18.

N.º 9.   N.º 9.

N.º 1.

N.º 6.   N.º 6.

N.º 8.   N.º 8.

N.º 15.

N.º 11.   N.º 11.

N.º 14.   N.º 14.

N.º 17.

N.º 18.

N.º 1.

N.º 4.   N.º 4.

N.º 5.   N.º 5.

N.º 15.

N.º 10.   N.º 10.

N.º 13.   N.º 13.

N.º 12.   N.º 12.

La colección de Historia Natural de ALBERTUS SEBA y su INVENTARIO GRÁFICO

IRMGARD MÜSCH

Albertus Seba, nacido en Etzel (Frisia oriental) en 1665, eligió la profesión de boticario, un oficio en aquel entonces estrechamente relacionado con los estudios de Historia Natural. En aquel tiempo, los medicamentos no se fabricaban sintéticamente como hoy en día, sino que se obtenían mezclando elementos naturales. Para conseguir las sustancias curativas de animales, plantas y minerales se disponía de toda una serie de recetas tradicionales. Sin embargo, muchos buscaban nuevas vías, coleccionaban objetos naturales de los cuatro puntos cardinales y estudiaban y ensayaban su posible aplicación. En muchos casos la pasión coleccionista e investigadora se emancipó del uso meramente farmacéutico; numerosos boticarios crearon colecciones de Historia Natural de consideración, contribuyendo así a un mejor conocimiento de la Naturaleza.

Con su comercio, que denominaba «La farmacopea alemana», Seba se granjeó pronto un gran prestigio. Al gran éxito de su botica, lo cual le permitió crear su extensa colección, contribuyó el hecho de que Seba fue un buen comerciante y no confió únicamente en clientes ocasionales; antes al contrario negoció con materias primas farmacéuticas (drogas) de fuera de Europa, para las que hacía publicidad –indicando el precio– en un periódico de Ámsterdam. Se ocupaba asimismo de la botica de viaje de los barcos que soltaban amarras en el puerto de dicha ciudad, así como de tratar a los marineros. Según la tradición, cuando un barco anclaba en el puerto, Seba se apresuraba a tratar a los marineros y conseguía comprar a buen precio los objetos que traían de lejanos países, o los obtenía por trueque con medicamentos.

Seba no pudo encontrar mejor lugar que Ámsterdam como base para crear una colección de Historia Natural; así reunió una colección cuyo prestigio llegaba hasta muy lejos de las fronteras de Ámsterdam.

EL THESAURUS DE ALBERTUS SEBA

El 30 de octubre de 1731 se cerró en Ámsterdam un acuerdo entre tres partes: los representantes de dos editoriales y Seba se pusieron de acuerdo para publicar el gabinete del coleccionista en una gran obra, acompañada de unos 400 cuadros. En realidad, el Thesaurus contiene nada menos que 446 tablas, 175 de ellas a doble plana. Los cuatro volúmenes de la obra se publicaron a lo largo de 30 años: de 1734 a 1765. Los textos explicativos de las ilustraciones aparecieron en dos versiones bilingües: en latín-francés y latín-neerlandés, pues Seba quería dirigirse con el Thesaurus a un público internacional de investigadores de la naturaleza, coleccionistas y amantes de los libros. Gran parte del texto del primer volumen lo escribió Seba mismo, si bien contó con la ayuda de otros investigadores. Al principio del primer volumen se encuentran unas páginas con ilustraciones de esqueletos de plantas, que Seba trató y conservó con una técnica especial. A continuación, el Thesaurus presenta representaciones de fauna y flora suramericana y asiática: junto a lagartos, pájaros, sapos, arañas y otros animales aparecen animales de fábula como dragones. El volumen II está dedicado principalmente a las serpientes; sin embargo, con fines decorativos y para ilustrar el modo de vida de los reptiles, se pueden ver algunas plantas y otros animales en las ilustraciones. El volumen III trata el ámbito vital acuático: el observador puede apreciar una gran variedad de animales del mar: moluscos, estrellas de mar, pulpos, erizos de mar y peces. El último volumen presenta, en casi 100 tablas, una nutrida colección de insectos, seguida de algunas páginas con representaciones de minerales y fósiles procedentes del gabinete de Seba.

La empresa de editar una obra como el Thesaurus exigió un amplio despliegue de medios económicos. Sobre todo las numerosas ilustraciones, cuya elaboración exigía mucho tiempo, causaron enormes gastos. Se conoce con su nombre a 13 artistas, que se ocuparon únicamente de trasladar a planchas las tablas, el frontispicio y el retrato. La costosa obra se publicó inicialmente en blanco y negro. No se sabe si las editoriales habían ofrecido también una edición coloreada, que naturalmente habría aumentado considerablemente el precio y el margen de beneficios. Es de suponer que los compradores la encargaran a especialistas en el coloreado, corriendo ellos con los gastos. La riqueza de color es un verdadero placer; pero el coloreado no solo elevaba el atractivo estético, sino también el valor científico. Por ejemplo, algunos ejemplares de mariposas, serpientes o moluscos solo se distinguen con la ayuda del color, mientras que en blanco y negro es muy difícil reconocer las diferencias entre algunos animales. Con o sin coloración, el Thesaurus es en cualquier caso un ejemplo impresionante del arte barroco de la imprenta. Las tablas de los volúmenes segundo a cuarto responden cada vez más a la presentación científica usual en aquella época. Los animales se presentan cuidadosamente clasificados por géneros. Para que las ilustraciones resulten lo más legibles posible se reproducen los animales sin interferencias y en una escala única; ahora bien, con los lados invertidos, lo cual -en el caso de los caracoles con la casa girada a la izquierda- produjo ciertos malentendidos. Se ha conservado la distribución ornamental de los objetos en las ilustraciones, como se aprecia tanto en la simetría de las tablas de serpientes como en la artística distribución de moluscos o insectos. De este modo, tanto las ilustraciones como la colección adquieren siempre un doble aspecto: sirven tanto para la formación científica como para el placer estético.

El Thesaurus divulgó un importante gabinete de Historia Natural de comienzos del siglo XVIII. La colección, en realidad fija, adquirió movilidad gracias a su publicación: muchas personas interesadas pudieron recurrir a ella, incluso cuando hacía ya decenios que la colección se había dispersado en todas las direcciones.

El presente volumen muestra una selección de los magníficos moluscos y corales del tercer volumen de la edición original.

22

de Treede Lade

P. Tanjé fecit.

TAB. XXXV.

Various mollusc shells arranged
as ornaments · Verschiedene
zu Ornamenten angeordnete
Gehäuse von Weichtieren ·
Arrangements ornementaux de
diverses coquilles de mollusques ·
Ornamentos formados por
conchas y moluscos

Various mollusc shells arranged as ornaments or garlands with pictorial motifs · Verschiedene zu Ornamenten und Girlanden mit bildhaften Motiven angeordnete Gehäuse von Schnecken und Muscheln · Arrangements ornementaux et en guirlandes de diverses coquilles de mollusques · Varias conchas de moluscos agrupadas formando conjuntos ornamentales y guirnaldas

TAB XXXVI.

de Derde Lade

Lade

26

de Vyfde

de Serde

TAB. XXXVII.

Ornaments made with mollusc
shells, depicting a stylised face ·
Ornamente aus Gehäusen von
Weichtieren mit Darstellung
eines stilisierten Gesichts ·
Arrangement ornemental
de coquilles de mollusques
représentant un visage stylisé ·
Ornamentos formados
por conchas y moluscos,
representando una cara estilizada

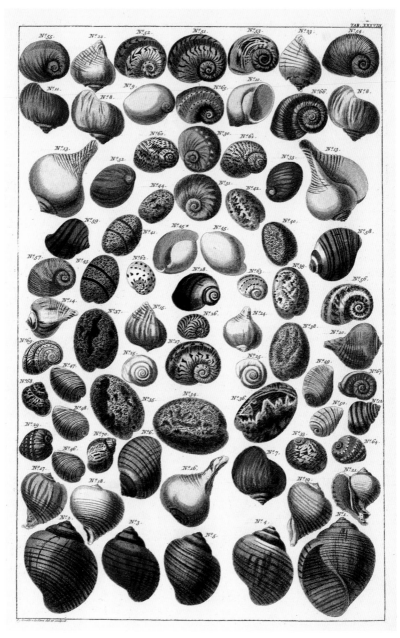

Rapa shells, moon shells, spiny conches and cephalaspidean opisthobranchs from the Indo-Pacific, African and American coastal regions · Kopfschild-, Nabel- und Stachelschnecken aus dem Indopazifik, afrikanischen und amerikanischen Küstengebieten · Coquilles de rapa, de natices, de murex et d'opisthobranches céphalaspidés de l'aire indopacifique et des zones côtières d'Afrique et d'Amérique · Rapa, caracol de luna y peonza rugosa del área indo-pacífico, y de las regiones costeras de África y América

Land, freshwater and sea shells from Europe, North America and Indo-Pacific · Land-, Süßwasser- und Meeresschnecken aus Europa, Nordamerika und dem Indopazifik · Mollusques marins, d'eau douce et terrestres d'Europe, d'Amérique du Nord et de l'aire indopacifique · Moluscos terrestres, de agua dulce y marinos de Europa, Norteamérica y área indo-pacífica

TAB. XL.

Land, freshwater and sea shells from Europe, Atlantic and Indo-Pacific · Land-, Süßwasser- und Meeresschnecken aus Europa, dem Atlantik und dem Indopazifik · Mollusques marins, d'eau douce et terrestres d'Europe, de l'Atlantique et de l'aire indopacifique · Moluscos terrestres, de agua dulce y marinos de Europa, Norteamérica y área indo-pacífica

TAB. XLIX.

Tritons, miter shells, nassas, and vase shells from the Indo-Pacific, Atlantic and Mediterranean Sea · Tritonshörner,
Giftwalzenschnecken, Netzreusenschnecken und Vasenschnecken aus dem Indopazifik, Atlantik und Mittelmeer ·
Tritons, cônes, mitres, nasses et vases de l'aire indopacifique, de l'Atlantique et de la mer Méditerranée ·
Tritones, conchas de mitras, nasarios y vasidae del área indo-pacífica, del Océano Atlántico y Mar Mediterráneo

TAB. XLI.

Nerites, top shells and moon shells from the Indo-Pacific, Atlantic and Mediterranean Sea ·
Schwimmschnecken, Spitzkreiselschnecken und Nabelschnecken aus dem Indopazifik, Atlantik und Mittelmeer ·
Nérites, troques (gibbules) et natices de l'aire indopacifique, de l'Atlantique et de la mer Méditerranée ·
Nerites, troques y náticas del área indo-pacífica, del Océano Atlántico y Mar Mediterráneo

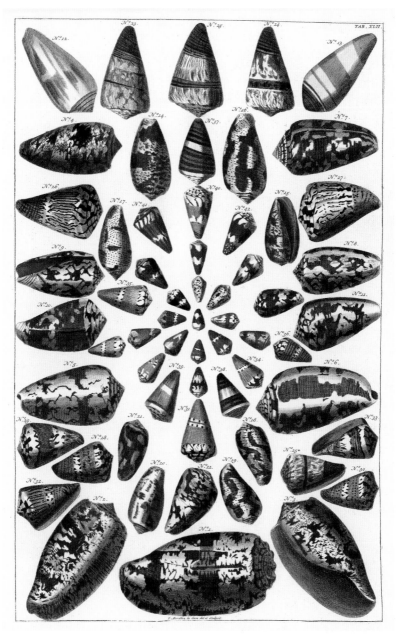

Poisonous cone shells, chiefly from the Indo-Pacific · Giftige Kegelschnecken, überwiegend aus dem Indopazifik ·
Cônes venimeux, originaires principalement de l'aire indopacifique · Conos venenosos, principalmente del área indo-pacífica

34

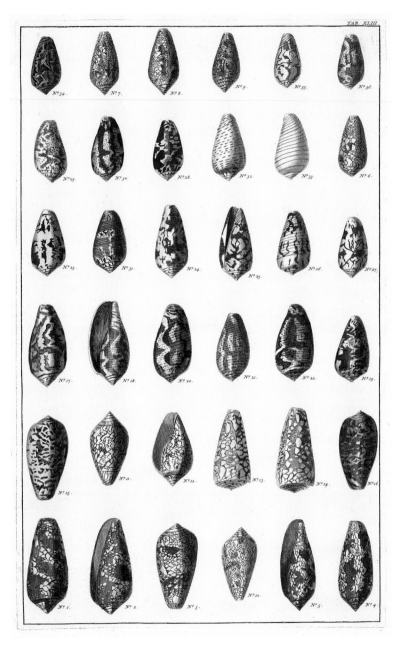

Poisonous cone shells, chiefly from the Indo-Pacific · Giftige Kegelschnecken, überwiegend aus dem Indopazifik ·
Cônes venimeux, originaires principalement de l'aire indopacifique · Conos venenosos, principalmente del área indo-pacífica

TAB. XLIV.

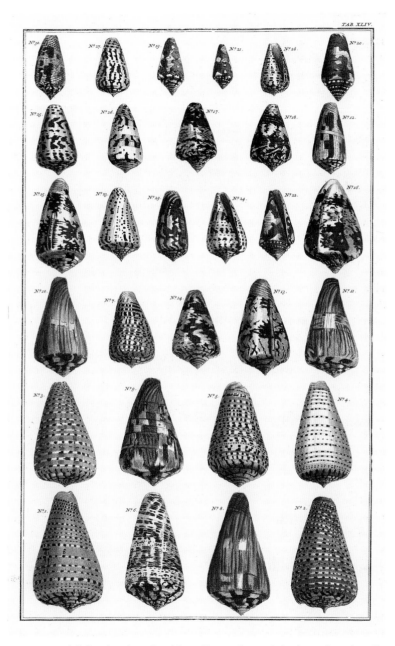

Poisonous cone shells from the Indo-Pacific and the Caribbean · Giftige Kegelschnecken aus dem Indopazifik
und der Karibik · Cônes venimeux, originaires principalement de l'aire indopacifique et des Caraïbes ·
Conos venenosos del área indo-pacífica y del Caribe

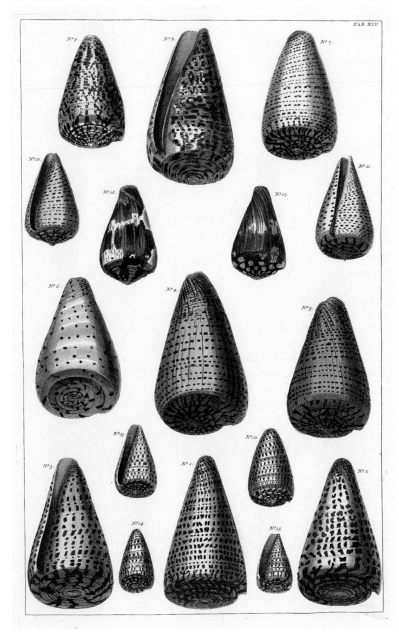

TAB. XLV.

Poisonous cone shells from tropical waters · Giftige Kegelschnecken aus tropischen Meeren ·
Cônes venimeux des mers tropicales · Conos venenosos de aguas tropicales

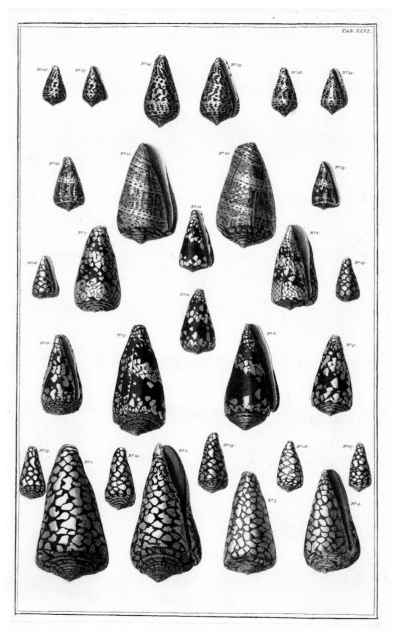

Poisonous cone shells, chiefly from the Indo-Pacific · Giftige Kegelschnecken, überwiegend aus dem Indopazifik ·
Cônes venimeux, originaires principalement de l'aire indopacifique · Conos venenosos, principalmente del área indo-pacífica

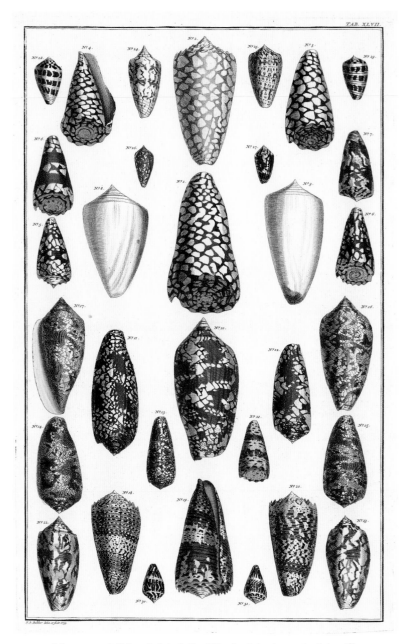

Poisonous cone shells from the Indo-Pacific · Giftige Kegelschnecken aus dem Indopazifik ·
Cônes venimeux, originaires de l'aire indopacifique · Conos venenosos del área indo-pacífica

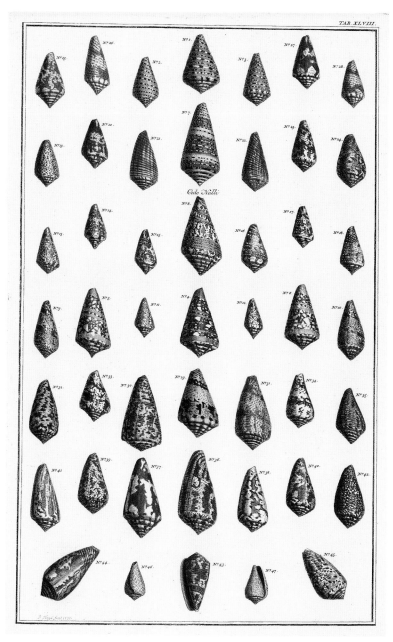

Cone shells from the Atlantic, Indian Ocean and Pacific · Kegelschnecken aus Atlantik,
Indischem Ozean und Pazifik · Cônes originaires de l'Atlantique, de l'océan Indien et du Pacifique ·
Conos venenosos de los océanos Atlántico, Índico y Pacífico

TAB. I.

Sea shells of different families from the Indo-Pacific · Meeresschnecken verschiedener Familien aus dem Indopazifik ·
Mollusques marins de différentes familles de l'aire indopacifique · Moluscos marinos de diferenctes familias del área indo-pacífica

TAB. LI.

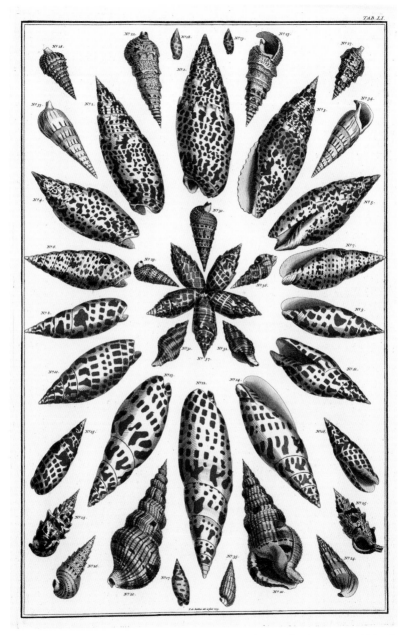

Miter shells, ceriths and a few other species from the Indo-Pacific · Bischofsmützenschnecken, Mitras, Nadelschnecken
und einige andere Arten aus dem Indopazifik · Mitres, cérinthes (cornets) et autres espèces de l'aire indopacifique ·
Mitras, Padas (Cerithiidae) y otras especies del área indo-pacífica

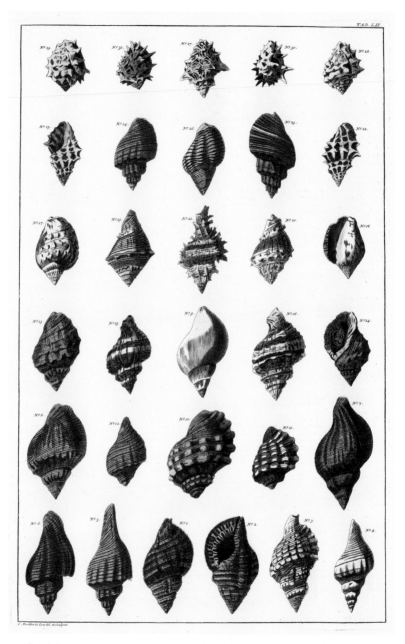

TAB. LII.

Sea snails, including murex shells and tritons, chiefly from the Indo-Pacific · Meeresschnecken, hauptsächlich aus dem Indopazifik, darunter Stachelschnecken und Tritonschnecken · Mollusques marins, incluant des murex et des tritons, principalement de l'aire indopacifique · Caracolas marinas, incluyendo murex y tritones, principalmente del área indo-pacífica

Tropical sea shells, including bonnet shells, mud shells, mudcreepers, olive shells, and cone shells · Tropische
Meeresschnecken, darunter Helmschnecken, Reusenschnecken, eine Turmdeckelschnecke, Olivenschnecken und
Kegelschnecken · Mollusques marins tropicaux, dont des casques, des nasses, un Thiaridae, des olives et des cônes ·
Moluscos marinos tropicales, incluyendo cascos, nasarios, una melanoides, olivas y conos

TAB. LIV.

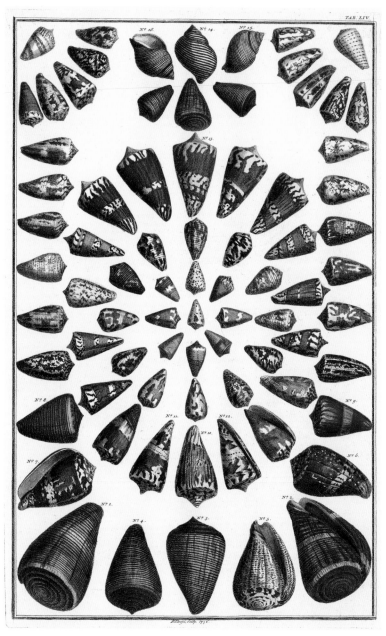

Poisonous cone shells and stone shells from tropical seas · Giftige Kegelschnecken und Spindelschnecken aus den tropischen Meeren · Cônes venimeux et fasciolariidés des mers des Tropiques · Conos venenosos y fascicolarias de los mares tropicales

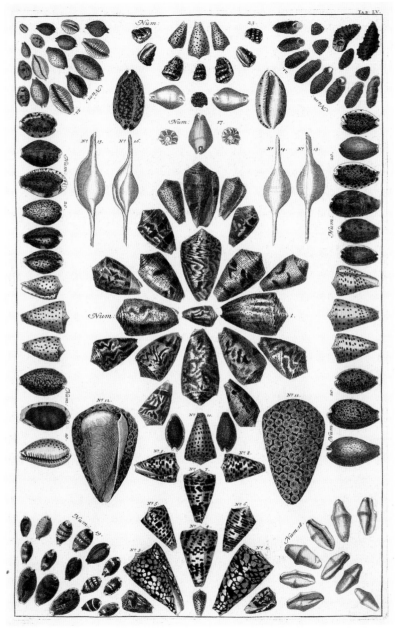

Cone shells and cowries from the Indo-Pacific and West Atlantic · Kegelschnecken und Porzellanschnecken
aus dem Indopazifik und dem Westatlantik · Cônes et porcelaines (cyrées et ovules) de l'aire indopacifique et
de l'Atlantique occidental · Conos y porcelanas (cipreas) del área indo-pacífica y del Atlántico occidental

TAB. LXI.

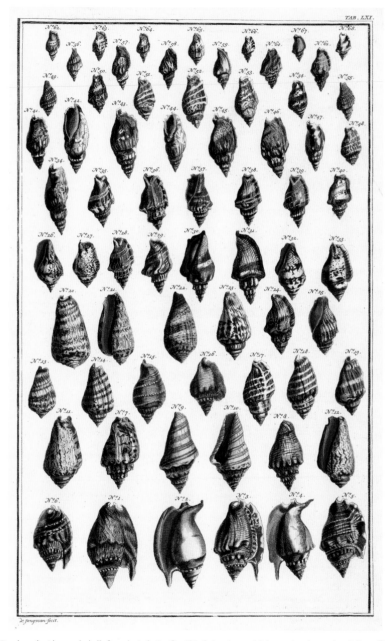

Conchs and spider conch shells from the Indo-Pacific · Flügelschnecken und Spinnenschnecke aus dem Indopazifik ·
Strombes et coquillage araignée de l'aire indopacifique · Strombus y conchas de chiragra del área indo-pacífica

TAB. LVI.

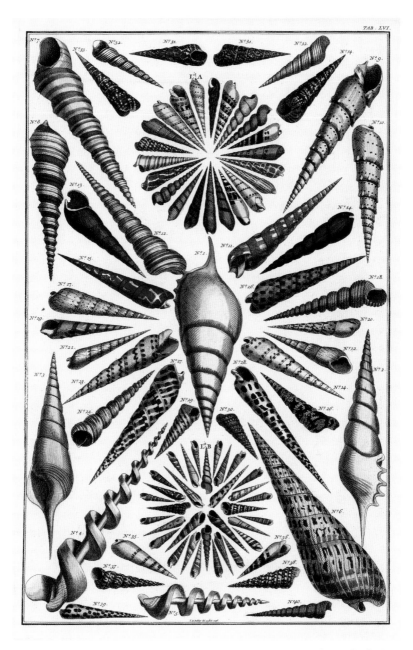

Turret shells, auger shells and tibias from the Indo-Pacific and the Caribbean · Indopazifische und karibische
Turmschnecken, Schraubenschnecken, Turmdeckelschnecken und Flügelschnecken · Turritelles, térèbres et tibias de
l'aire indopacifique et des Caraïbes · Torrecillas (turritellidae), terebras y tibias del área indo-pacífica y del Caribe

TAB. LVII.

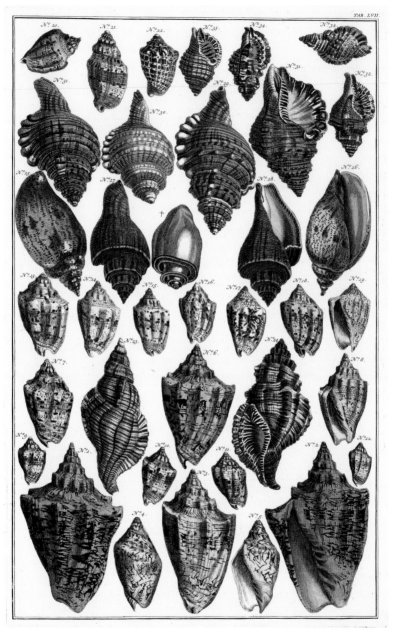

Volutes, tritons and giant hairy melongena from the Pacific, West Atlantic and the South Indian coastal region ·
Walzenschnecken, Tritonshörner und Kronenschnecken aus dem Pazifik, Westatlantik und der südindischen Küstenregion ·
Volutes, tritons et mélongénidés du Pacifique, de l'Atlantique occidental et de la région côtière du sud de l'Inde ·
Volutas, tritones y melongena negra del Pacífico, del Atlántico y de la región costera del sur de la India

Nerite shells and moon shells · Schwimmschnecken und Nabelschnecken · Nérites et natices · Nerites y náticas

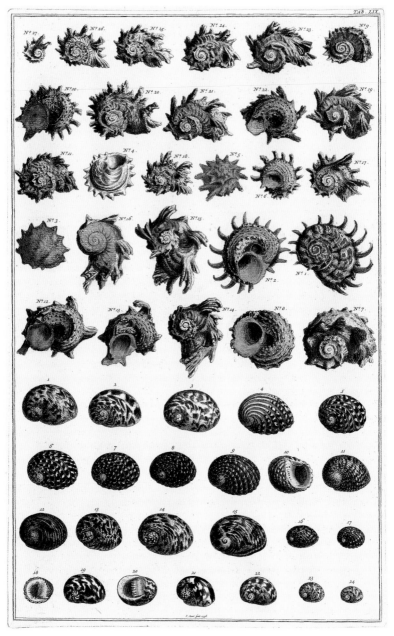

TAB. LIX.

Nerite shells, star shells and angaria shells from the Indo-Pacific and West Atlantic · Schwimmschnecken,
Kreiselschnecken und Stachelschnecken aus dem Indopazifik und dem Westatlantik · Nérites, astreas et anarias de l'aire
indopacifique et de l'Atlantique occidental · Nerites, astreas y anarias del área indo-pacífica y del Atlántico occidental

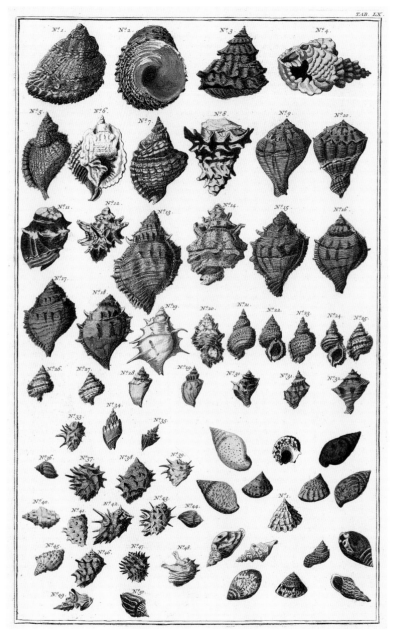

Star shells, periwinkles, tritons, vase shells, murex shells and conchs from the Indo-Pacific and West Atlantic ·
Kreiselschnecken, Strandschnecken, Tritonshörner, Vasenschnecken, Stachelschnecken und Flügelschnecken
aus dem Indopazifik und Westatlantik · Astreas, bigorneaux, tritons, vases, murex et strombes de l'aire indopacifique
et de l'Atlantique occidental · Astreas, bígaros, tritones, murex y strombus del área indo-pacífica y del Atlántico

52

N.º 47.   N.º 26.   N.º 42.   N.º 38.

N.º 41.   N.º 27.

N.º 32.   N.º 40.

N.º 20.   N.º 35.

N.º 46.   N.º 11.

N.º 35.   N.º 30.

N.º 22.   N.º 34.

N.º 9.   N.º 8.   N.º 6.

N.º 22.   N.º 18.

N.º 48.

N.º 4.   N.º 3.

N.º 1.   N.º 27.   N.º 28.

F. de Bakker del. et Sculp. 1758.

TAB. LXII.

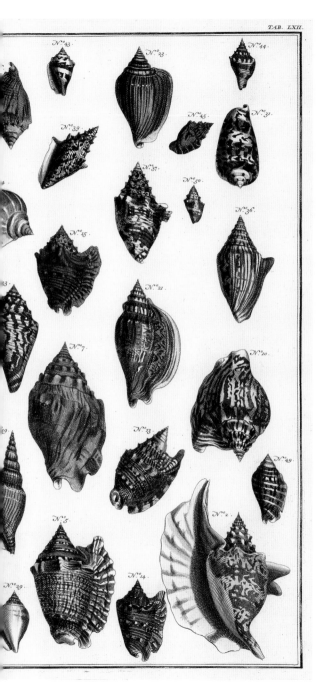

Conchs, spider conch shells
and the common pelican's foot ·
Flügelschnecken, Spinnenschnecken
und der Pelikanfuß · Strombes,
coquillages araignées et pied de
pélican · Strombus, conchas de
chiragra y pie de pelícano común

TAB. LXIII.

Chiefly conchs from tropical seas · Hauptsächlich Flügelschnecken aus tropischen Meeren ·
Principalement des strombes des mers tropicales · Principalmente strombus de mares tropicales

TAB. LXIV

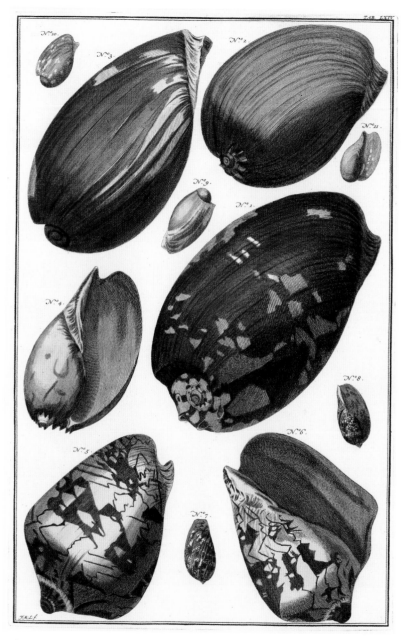

Volutes from the tropical seas around Australia, Indonesia and West Africa · Walzenschnecken aus den tropischen
Meeren bei Australien, Indonesien und Westafrika · Volutes des mers tropicales de l'Australie, de l'Indonésie
et de l'Afrique occidentale · Volutas de los mares tropicales de Australia, Indonesia y África occidental

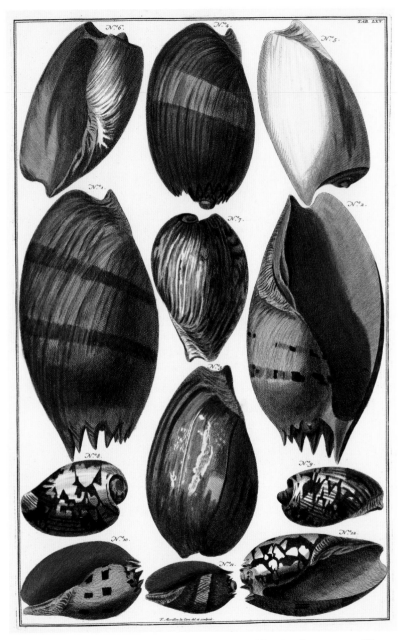

TAB. LXV

Volutes from the Indo-West Pacific near Australia and Indonesia, and from the Atlantic near West Africa ·
Walzenschnecken aus dem Indo-Westpazifik bei Australien und Indonesien, und aus dem Atlantik bei Westafrika ·
Volutes de l'aire indopacifique, près de l'Australie et de l'Indonésie, ainsi que de l'Atlantique près de l'Afrique occidentale ·
Volutas del área indo-pacífica, cerca de Australia e Indonesia, así como del Atlántico cerca de África occidental

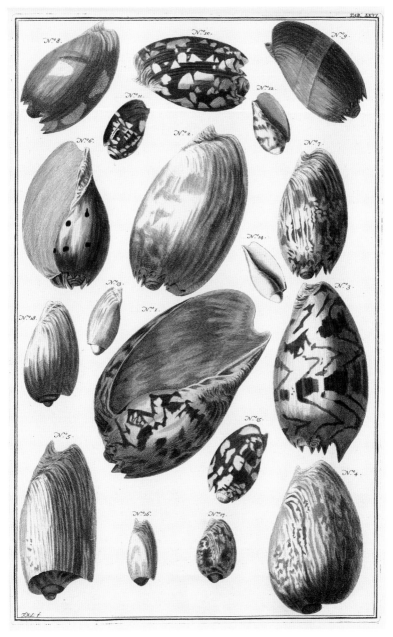

Volutes from the tropical seas near West Africa, Indonesia and Australia · Walzenschnecken aus den tropischen Meeren
bei Westafrika, Indonesien und Australien · Volutes des mers tropicales près de l'Afrique occidentale,
de l'Indonésie et de l'Australie · Volutas de los mares tropicales cerca de África occidental, Indonesia y Australia

TAB. LXVII.

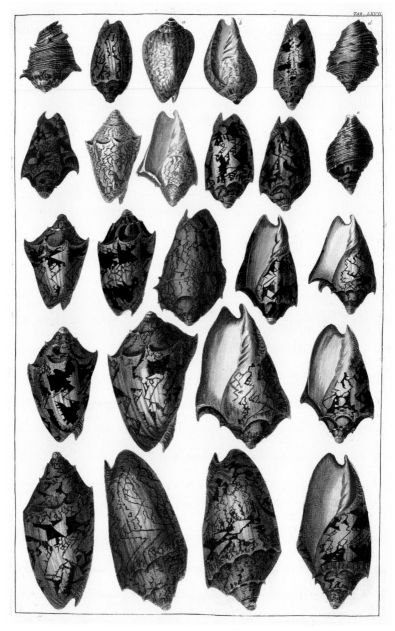

Volutes from tropical seas · Walzenschnecken aus den tropischen Meeren ·
Volutes des mers tropicales · Volutas de los mares tropicales

TAB. LXVIII.

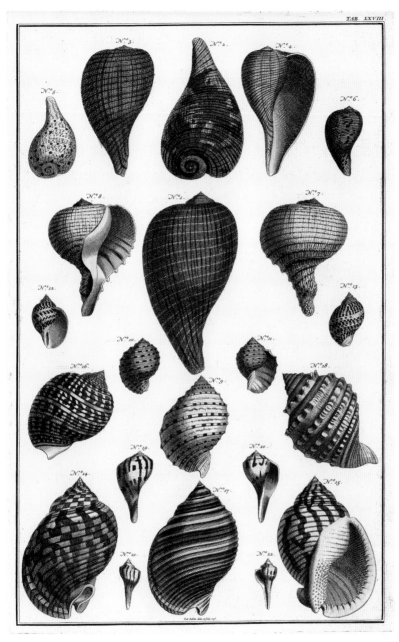

Tun shells, helmet shells, fig shells and other sea shells from North-East America, the Mediterranean, the Indo-West Pacific ·
Tonnen-, Helm-, Feigen- und andere Meeresschnecken aus Nordost-Amerika, dem Mittelmeer, dem Indo-Westpazifik · Tonnes, casques, figues et a autres mollusques marins du nord-est de l'Amérique, de la mer Méditerranée et de l'océan Indien et Pacifique occidental · Moluscos marinos del noreste de América, del Mar Mediterráneo y de los océanos Índico y Pacífico occidental

TAB. LXIX.

Tun shells and helmet shells from
the Indo-Pacific and West Atlantic ·
Tonnenschnecken und Helmschnecken
aus dem Indopazifik und dem Westatlantik · Tonnes et casques de l'aire
indopacifique et de l'Atlantique
occidental · Tonnidae y cascos del área
indo-pacífica y del Atlántico occidental

TAB. LXX.

Tun shells, helmet shells and harp shells from the Indo-Pacific, the Caribbean and the Mediterranean Sea ·
Tonnenschnecken, Helmschnecken und Harfenschnecken aus dem Indopazifik, der Karibik und dem Mittelmeer ·
Tonnes, casques et harpes de l'aire indopacifique, des Caraïbes et de la mer Méditerranée ·
Tonnidae, cascos y arpas del área indo-pacífica, del Caribe y del Mar Mediterráneo

Helmet shells and sea shells from the Indo-Pacific, the Atlantic, the Caribbean and the Mediterranean Sea ·
Helmschnecken und Meeresschnecken aus dem Indopazifik, dem Atlantik, der Karibik und dem Mittelmeer ·
Casques et mollusques marins de l'aire indopacifique, de l'Atlantique, des Caraïbes et de la mer Méditerranée ·
Moluscos marinos del área indo-pacífica, del Atlántico, del Caribe y del Mar Mediterráneo

Spindle shells and helmet shells from the Indo-Pacific and the Caribbean, and land snails from Africa and South America · Meeresschnecken der Familien Fasciolariidae und Cassidae aus dem Indopazifik und der Karibik, sowie Landschnecken aus Afrika und Südamerika · Fuseaux et casques de l'aire indopacifique et de la mer des Caraïbes, ainsi que des mollusques terrestres (achatines et bulimes) d'Afrique et d'Amérique du Sud · Fascicolarias, cascos del área indo-pacífica y del Caribe, así como moluscos terrestres de África y de América del Sur

TAB. LXXI.

TAB. LXXIII.

Helmet shells, cone shell and whelks
from the Indo-Pacific, West Africa
and the Caribbean · Helmschnecken,
Kegelschnecke und Wellhorn-
schnecken aus dem Indopazifik,
Westafrika und der Karibik ·
Casques, cône et buccins de l'aire
indopacifique, de l'Afrique occidentale et des Caraïbes · Cascos, conos
y buccinos del área indo-pacífica,
de África occidental y del Caribe

TAB. LXXIV.

Turban shells from the Indo-Pacific, the West Atlantic and the South African coastal region · Turbanschnecken aus dem
Indopazifik, Westatlantik und der südafrikanischen Küstenregion · Turbos de l'aire indopacifique, de l'Atlantique
occidental et du littoral sud-africain · Turbos del área indo-pacífica, del Atlántico occidental y del litoral sudafricano

TAB. LXXVI.

Cowries and egg shells from the Indo-Pacific · Kauris und Eierschnecken aus dem Indopazifik ·
Cauries et porcelaines de l'aire indopacifique · Porcelanas y cipreas del área indo-pacífica

TAB. LXXVII

Murex shells, chiefly from the Indo-Pacific · Stachelschnecken der Familie Muricidae, hauptsächlich aus dem Indopazifik · Murex (ou rochers), principalement de l'aire indopacifique · Murex, principalmente del área indo-pacífica

TAB. LXXVIII

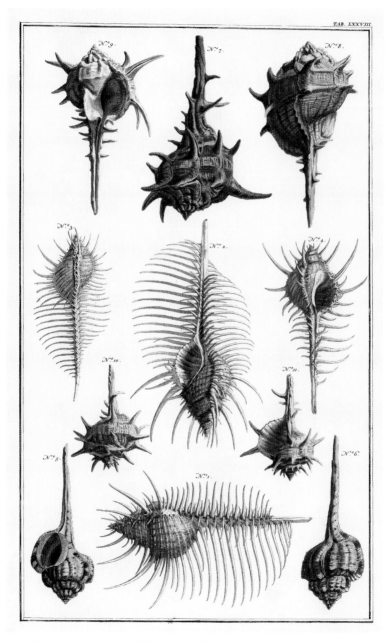

Murex shells from the Indo-Pacific, West Africa and the Mediterranean Sea · Stachelschnecken der Familie Muricidae
aus dem Indopazifik, Westafrika und dem Mittelmeer · Murex peignes et autres murex de l'aire indopacifique, de l'Afrique
occidentale et de la mer Méditerranée · Murex del área indo-pacífica, de África occidental y del Mar Mediterráneo

72

Slit shell, top shells, and turban shells ·
Schlitzbandschnecke, Spitzkreisel-
schnecken und Turbanschnecken ·
Pleurotomaire, troques et turbos ·
Pleurotomaria, troques y turbos

TAB. LXXIX

A. Vanderlaan fec.

Spindles, crown shells and turrid shells
from tropical seas · Spindelschnecken,
Kronenschnecken und Turmschnecken
aus tropischen Meeren · Fasciolaires
ou fuseaux, mélongenidés et turridés
des eaux tropicales · Fascicolarias,
melongenidae y turridae de aguas
tropicales

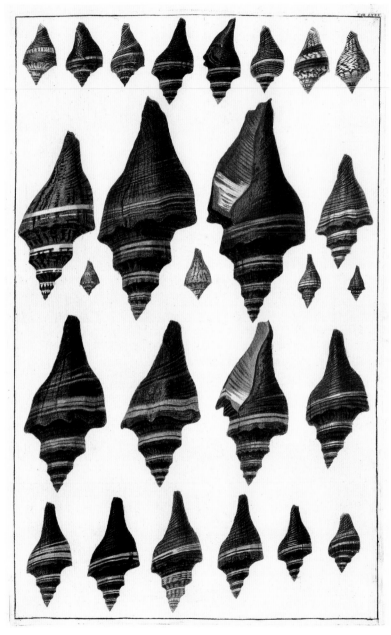

Melongenids from tropical waters · Kronenschnecken aus tropischen Gewässern ·
Mélongénidés des eaux tropicales · Melongenidae de aguas tropicales

Juvenile spider conchs (Strombidae family) from the Indo-Pacific, and two species of whelk from the northern Atlantic ·
Jungtiere von Spinnenschnecken der Familie Strombidae aus dem Indopazifik und zwei Wellhornschnecken-Arten aus dem
Nordatlantik · Jeunes coquillages araignées ou lambris (famille des Strombidae) de l'aire indopacifique et deux espèces
de buccin de l'Atlantique Nord · Jóvenes chiragras del área indo-pacífica y dos especies de buccinos del Atlántico norte

P. Tanjé fecit.

TAB. LXXXI.

79

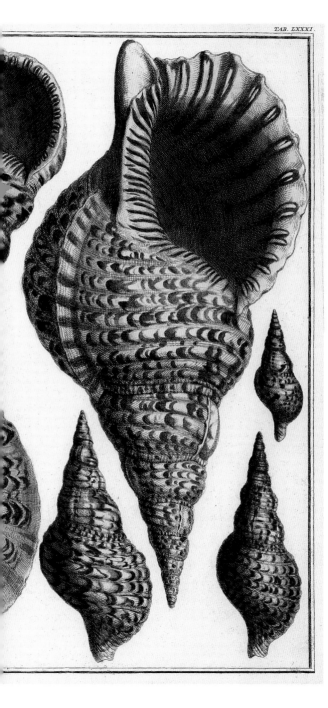

Triton trumpets · Tritonshörner ·
Grands tritons · Grandes tritones

Spider conchs or lambis shells
(Strombidae family), from the
Indo-Pacific · Spinnenschnecken
der Familie Strombidae aus dem
Indopazifik · Coquillages araignées
ou lambis (famille des Strombidae)
de l'aire indopacifique · Chiragras
o Strombus (familia Strombidae) del
área indo-pacífica

TAB. LXXXII.

1-3 Chambered nautilus /Pearly
nautilus (etched) · Perlboote
(graviert) · Nautiles (décorés et
gravés) · Cámara de nautilo/nautilo
nacarado (grabado) 4-12 Paper
nautilus · Papierboote · Argonautes ·
Argonautas

Drawings etched into the mother-of-pearl plates of Nautilus · Ritzzeichnungen auf Perlmuttplättchen von Nautilus Dessins gravés dans de la nacre de nautile · Dibujos grabados en planchas nacaradas de nautilo

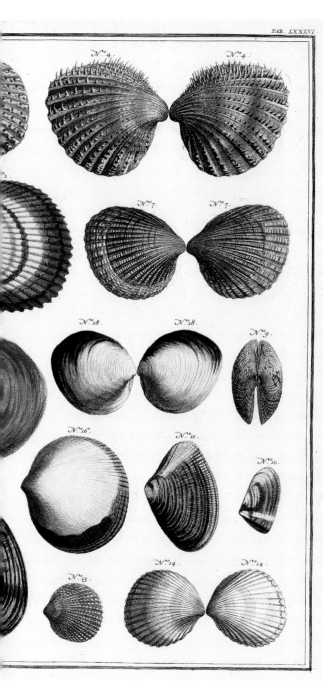

Ox heart, cockles, donax shells and
ocean quahog from the Atlantic,
Mediterranean Sea and the Indo-
Pacific · Ochsenherz, Herz-
muscheln, Donaxmuscheln und
Islandmuscheln aus dem Atlantik,
Mittelmeer und Indopazifik ·
Cœur de bœuf, coques ou
cardiidés, donax et cyprines
nordiques de l'Atlantique, de
la mer Méditerranée et de l'aire
indopacifique · Corazón de buey,
berberechos, donax y cyprina
islándica del Atlántico, del Mar
Mediterráneo y del área indo-
pacífica

88

Thorny oysters, Lazarus jewel boxes and an ark shell from the West Atlantic, Mediterranean Sea and the Indo-Pacific · Stachelaustern, Lazarus-Schmuckkästchen und Archenmuschel aus dem Westatlantik, Mittelmeer und Indopazifik · Spondyles pieds d'âne, chames lazarus et ache barbue de l'Atlantique occidental, de la mer Méditerranée et de l'aire indopacifique · Ostras rojas (Spondylidae), joyeros de Lázaro y anadara del Atlántico occidental, Mar Mediterráneo y área indo-pacífica

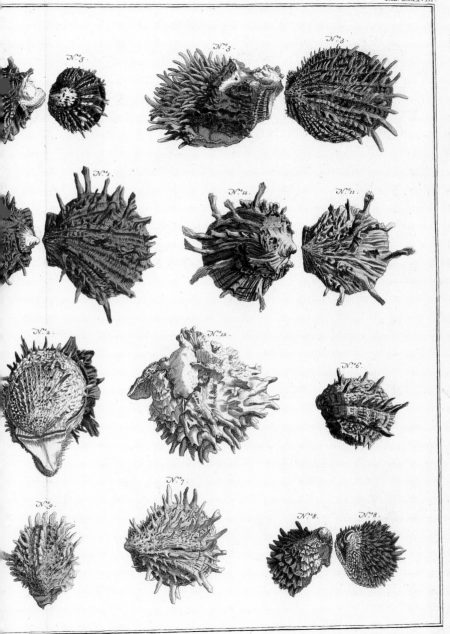

N.º 3.   N.º 1.   N.º 2.

N.º 5.   N.º 6.   N.º 4.

N.º 7.   N.º 7.   N.º 9.

N.º 10.

N.º 11.   N.º 11.

Thorny oysters, Lazarus jewel boxes
and a coral from the Indo-Pacific ·
Stachelaustern, Lazarus-Schmuckkästchen und eine Koralle aus dem
Indopazifik · Spondyles pieds d'âne,
chames lazarus et un corail de l'aire
indopacifique · Ostras rojas (Spondylidae), joyeros de Lázaro y un coral
del área indo-pacífica

Scallops from the West Atlantic
and the Indo-Pacific · Kamm-
muscheln aus dem Westatlantik
und Indopazifik · Peignes
de l'Atlantique occidental et
de l'aire indopacifique · Zambu-
riñas del Atlántico occidental
y del área indo-pacífica

TAB. LXXXVII.

93

Mussels, oysters and European jingle
shells from the Indo-Pacific, Atlantic
and Mediterranean Sea · Muscheln,
Austern und Europäische Sattelaustern
aus dem Indopazifik, Atlantik und
Mittelmeer · Coquillages, huîtres
et anomie pelure d'oignon, de l'aire
indopacifique, de l'Atlantique et de
la mer Méditerranée · Moluscos,
ostras y Anomiidae europeas del área
indo-pacífica, del Océano Atlántico
y del Mar Mediterráneo

TAB. XC.

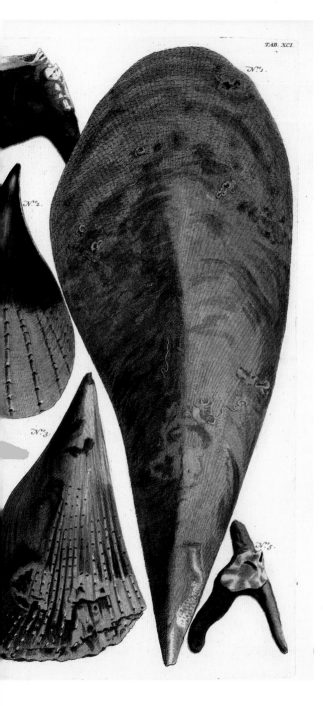

TAB. XCI.

Nº 1.

Nº 2.

Nº 3.

Nº 5.

Noble Pen shells and other pen
shells, hammer oysters and tree
oysters from the Mediterranean Sea,
Indo-Pacific and West Atlantic ·
Steckmuscheln, Hammermuscheln
und Flügelmuscheln aus dem Mittelmeer, Indopazifik und Westatlantik ·
Jambonneau hérissé, malleus et
autres huîtres nacrées de la mer
Méditerranée, l'aire ndopacifique
et de l'Atlantique occidental ·
Pínnidos, malleus y ostras nacaradas
(pteriidae) del Mar Mediterráneo,
del área indo-pacífica y del Atlántico
occidental

Prickly pen shells and rude pen
shells from the Indian Ocean,
Atlantic and Mediterranean Sea ·
Steckmuscheln aus dem Indischen
Ozean, Atlantik und Mittelmeer ·
Pinnes de l'océan Indien, de l'Atlan-
tique et de la mer Méditerranée ·
Pinnidae de los océanos Índico y
Atlántico y del Mar Mediterráneo

TAB. XCIII

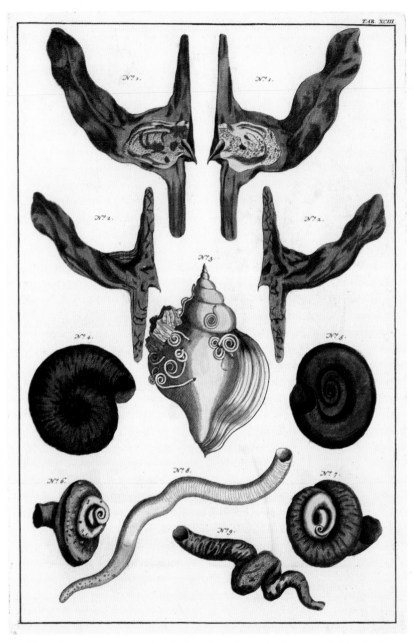

Common hammer oysters, neptune shell with barnacles, ramshorn snail, and sea worm tubes (Serpulidae) ·
Hammermuscheln, Neptunschnecke mit Seepocken, Posthornschnecke und Wohnröhren von Borstenwürmern ·
Malleus/marteaux, buccins avec des balanes et des serpules, planorbes d'eau douce, et tubes de vers serpulidés (chétopodes) ·
Malleus comunes, concha de Neptuno con percebes, caracol carnero y tubos de poliquetos

1 Finger sponge · Fingerschwamm · Eponge · Esponja 2 Staghorn sponge · Geweihschwamm · Eponge · Esponja
3 Sponge oceanopia · Schwamm · Eponge · Esponja 4 Breadcrumb sponge · Brotkrumenschwamm ·
Eponge mie de pain · Esponja 6 Hornwrack · Blättermoostier · Bryozoaires foliacés · Briozoarios foliados

1, 7 Yellow tube sponges · Neptunschwämme · Eponges · Esponjas (Copa de Neptuno) **2, 4** Venus sea fans · Venusfächer · Corbeilles de Vénus ou gorgone · Abanico de Venus **3** Finger sponge · Fingerschwamm · Eponge · Esponja **8** Chalice sponge · Venusfächer · Corbeille de Vénus ou gorgone · Esponja de la clase Demospongiae **9** Staghorn sponge · Höckriger Geweihschwamm · Eponge · Axinella Cannabina

TAB. XCV.

N.ᵒ 1.

N.ᵒ 4.

N.ᵒ 8.

N.ᵒ 9.

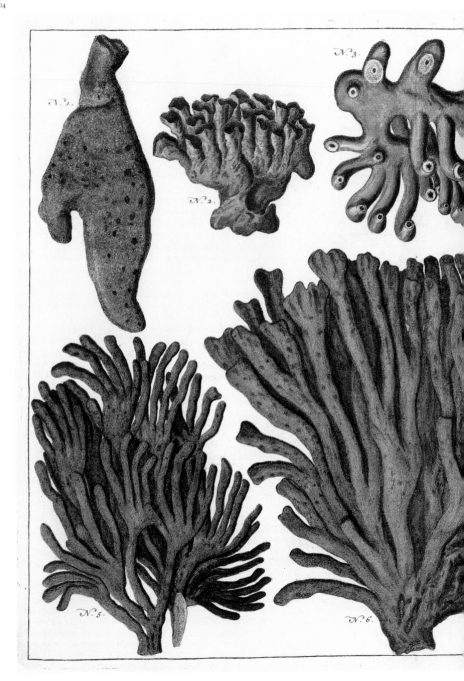

N.º 1.

N.º 2.

N.º 3.

N.º 5.

N.º 6.

TAB. XCVII.

N.º 4.

N.º 7.

1 Fan sponge · Schwamm · Eponge ·
Phakellia flabellata 2 Colonial ane-
mone · Krustenanemone · Anémone
encroûtante · Anémona incrustante
amarilla 4 Flesh sponge · Fleisch-
schwamm · Eponge bleue · Esponja
5-7 Eyed finger sponges/Mermaid's
gloves · Geweihschwamm · Chalines/
Eponges pourpres · Esponjas púrpuras

TAB. C.

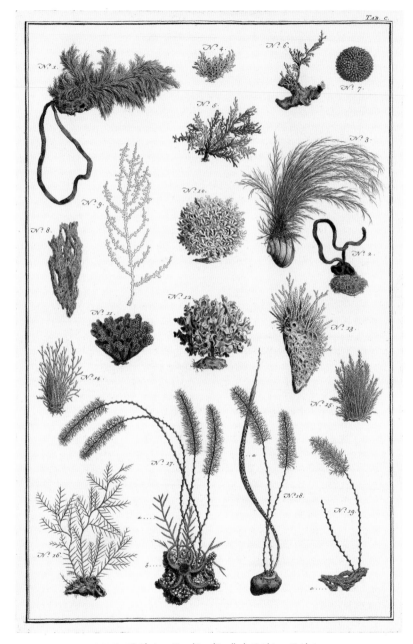

I, II, 16-19 Cnidarians · Nesseltiere (Korallen) · Cnidaires · Cnidarias
2, 9-10, 12 Moss animals · Moostiere · Bryozoaires · Briozoarios **8** Sea worm · Röhrenwurm · Salmacine · Sabellia sp.
13-15 Coral weeds · Korallenmoos · Coralito · Algues **17b** Serpent star · Schlangenstern · Ophiure · Ophiomyxa species
17a, 18-19 Bottle brushes · Flaschenputzer Hydroiden · Hydraires · Hidroidos

TAB. CI.

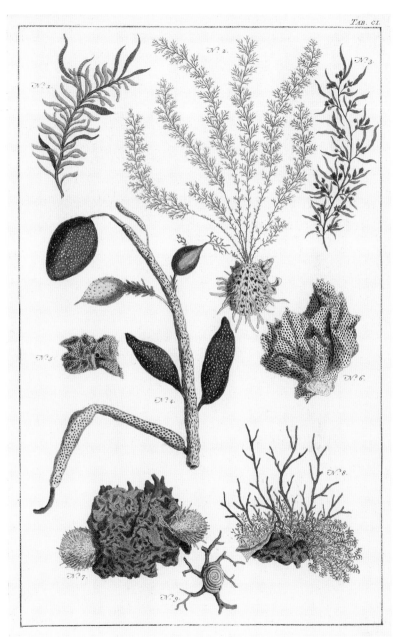

1 Cnidarian · Nesseltier (Koralle) · Cnidaire · Cnidarias 2 White weed · Zypressenmoos · Hydroïde · Sertularia cupressina
3 Sea plant · Meeresalge · Plante marine · Planta marina 5-6 Sea laces (Moss animals) · Neptunsschleier · Dentelles de
Neptune (Bryozoaires) · Encajes de Neptuno 8 Precious coral with hydroids · Edelkoralle mit Hydroiden · Corail rouge
et hydroïde · Corales rojos con Hidroidos 9 Staghorn bryozoan · Hirschgeweihmoostierchen · Bryozoaire · Briozoarios

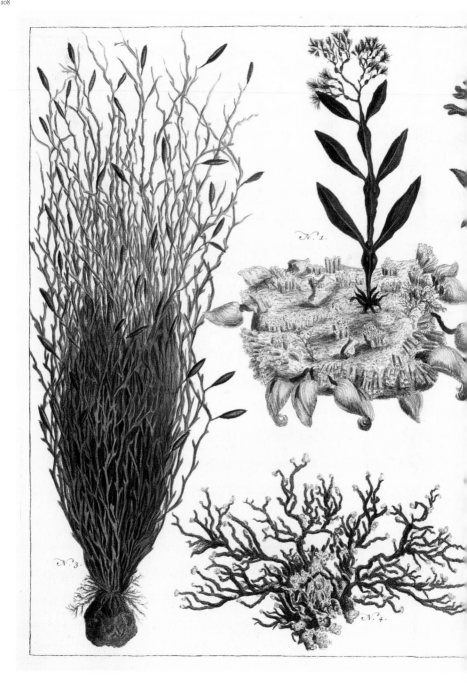

TAB. XCVIII.

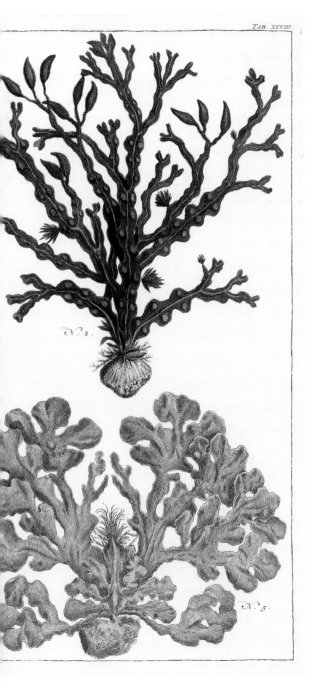

N.° 2.

N.° 5.

1-3 Sea plants · Meeresalgen · Plantes de
la mer · Plantas marinas **4** Gelatinous
bryozoan · Gallertmoostier · Bryozoaire
gélatineux · Briozoario gelatinoso
5 Moss animal · Korallenmoostier ·
Bryozoaire · Briozoario

N.1.

N.

TAB. CIV.

1 Carnation coral · Rote Lederkoralle ·
Corail mou · Coral (Dendronephthya)
2 Black coral · Schwarze Gorgonie ·
Corail noir · Coral negro

TAB. CV.

N.° 3.

N.° 4.

1-4 Cnidarians · Nesseltiere
(Korallen) · Cnidaires · Cnidarias
1a Sea whip · Seepeitsche · Fouet
de mer · Azote de mar **1b** Violescent
sea whip · Rote Gorgonie · Gorgone
rouge · Gorgona roja

114

1-4, 6-8 Cnidarians · Nesseltiere
(Korallen) · Cnidaires · Cnidarias
1 Hydroid · Hydroid · Hydroïde ·
Hidroidos 2 Bottlebrush hydroid ·
Flaschenbürstenmoos · Cnidaire
hydroïde · Cnidaria hidroida
3 Pink sea fan · Warzenkoralle ·
Gorgone rosée · Gorgona rosada
4 Sea whip · Rumphella Koralle ·
Gorgone rumphella · Gorgona
rumphella 6 Cnidarian with a
thorny oyster · Nesseltier (Koralle)
mit Stachelauster · Cnidaire avec
un mollusque spondyle · Cnidaria
con una ostra roja 7 Flower head ·
Röhrenpolyp · Tubulaire · Tubula-
ria 8 Fire coral · Feuerkoralle ·
Corail de feu · Millepora

N.º 3.

N.º 4.

N.º 7.

N.º 8.

N.º 9.

P. Tanji fecit. 1731.

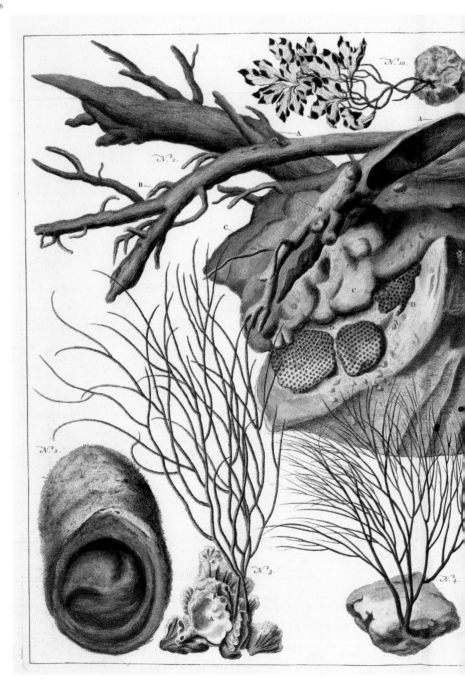

TAB. CVII.

N.º 8.

N.º 9.

N.º 7.

N.º 6.

N.º 5.

3-6, 8 Cnidarians · Nesseltiere
(Korallen) · Cnidaires · Cnidarias
3 Orange gorgonian · Orangerote
Gorgonie · Gorgone orange ·
Gorgona naranja **4** Sea whip ·
Seepeitsche · Fouet de mer ·
Gorgona rumphella **6** Violescent
sea whip · Rote Gorgonie · Gorgone
rouge · Gorgona roja **8** Feathery
black coral · Schwarze Koralle ·
Corail noir · Coral negro **9** Caulerpa · Caulerpa · Caulerpa · Caulerpa

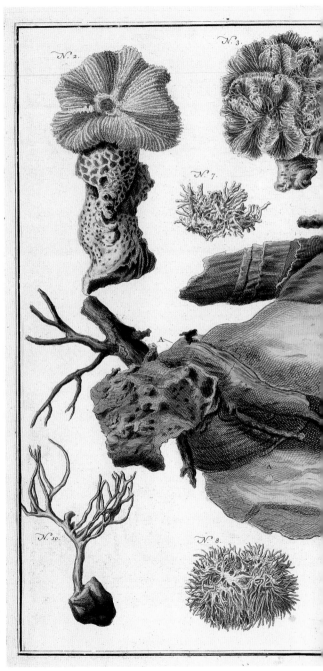

2-11 Cnidarians · Nesseltiere
(Korallen) · Cnidaires · Cnidarias
2, 4 Toadstools · Pilzlederkorallen ·
Corail cuir · Corales de cuero
3, 5 Open brain corals · Wulst-
korallen · Trachyphyllidés/coraux
cerveaux · Trachiphyllia sp
6 Raspberry coral · Himbeerkoralle ·
Corail *Pocillopora damicornis* · Coral
de tallo marrón 8 Needle coral ·
Nadelkoralle · Corail seriatopora ·
Seriatopora calendrum 9 Cup coral ·
Kelchkoralle · Corail stelliforme ·
Coral copa 10 Cnidarian · Nesseltier
(Koralle) · Cnidaire · Cnidaria
11 Gorgonian · Gorgonie · Gorgone ·
Gorgona

TAB. CX.

1-10 Cnidarians · Nesseltiere
(Korallen) · Cnidaires · Cnidarias
1-2 Golden sea fans · Goldene
Seefächer/Königsgliederkorallen ·
Coraux dorés · Corales dorados
3 Smooth flower coral · Glatte
Blumenkoralle · Corail fleur · Coral
flor **6** Lettuce coral & plate corals ·
Salatkoralle & Pilzkorallen · Tubi-
naire jaune & coraux champignons ·
Turbinaria & Heliofungia **7** Fire
coral · Brettartige Feuerkoralle ·
Corail feu en plaque · Millepora
8-9 Organ pipe corals · Orgel-
korallen · Tubipore ou orgue de
mer · Clavularias

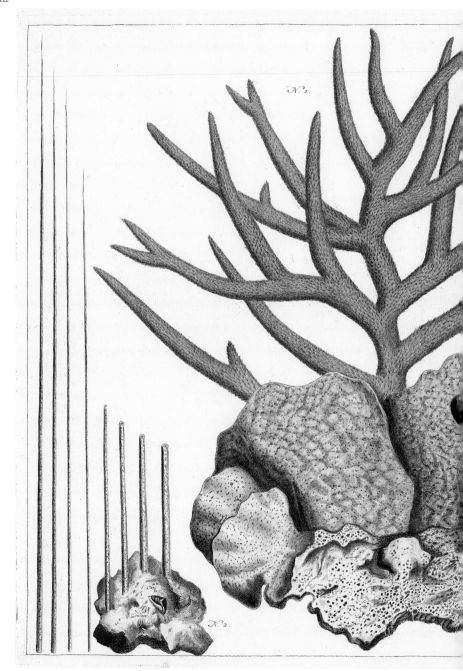

TAB. CXIV.

N.º 3.

1-2 Cnidarians · Nesseltiere
(Korallen) · Cnidaires · Cnidarias
1 Staghorn coral · Geweihkoralle ·
Corail bois · Acroporas
3 Mediterranean feather star ·
Mittelmeerhaarstern · Lys de mer
de Méditerranée · Comátula
mediterránea

TAB. CXV.

N.º 3.

N.º 7.

N.º 6.

1-7 Precious corals · Edelkorallen ·
Coraux rouges · Corales rojos

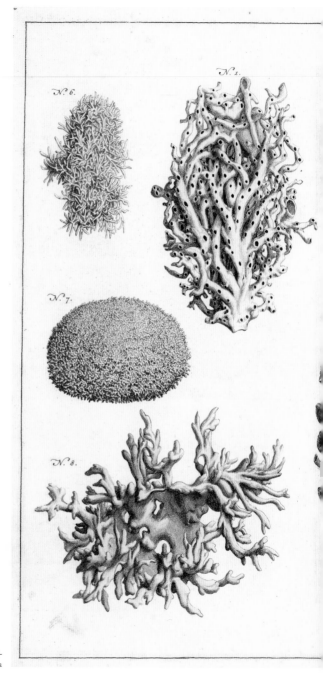

1-8 Cnidarians · Nesseltiere
(Korallen) · Cnidaires · Cnidarias
1-2 Ocular corals · Augenkorallen ·
Coraux blancs · Corales blancos
4 Star coral · Sternkoralle · Corail
étoile · Coral estrella 5 Staghorn
coral · Geweihkoralle · Corail bois ·
Acroporas 6 Needle coral · Nadelkoralle · Corail seriatopora · Seriatopora

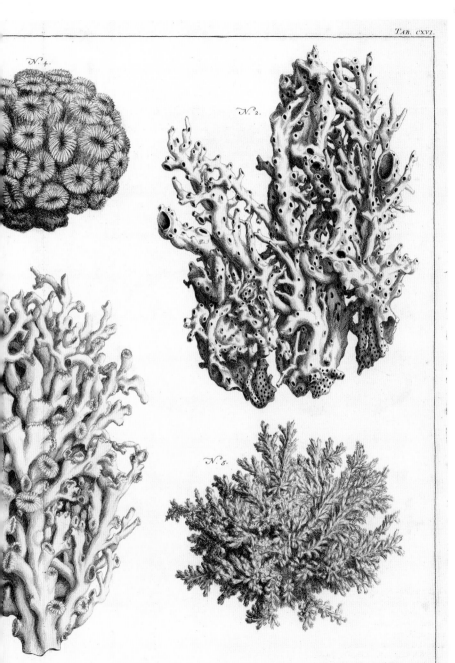

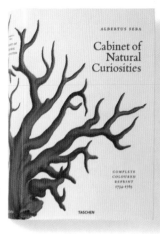

Albertus Seba
Cabinet of Natural Curiosities
Irmgard Müsch, Jes Rust, Rainer Willmann /
Hardcover, 636 pp. /
€ 200 / $ 200 / £ 135 / ¥ 25.000

"This is a massive book. It is also, probably, one of the most beautiful you are ever likely to see." —*Fortean Times*, London

"Buy them all and add some pleasure to your life."

ICONS

N.⁴4.

N.⁵5.